HARRY CAN HEAR

written by Fynisa Engler
illustrated by Milanka Reardon

This edition first published in 2023
by Lawley Publishing,
a division of Lawley Enterprises LLC.

Hardcover ISBN 978-1-956357-96-7
Paperback ISBN 978-1-956357-98-1
Library of Congress Control Number: 2022940762

Lawley Publishing
70 S. Val Vista Dr. #A3 #188
Gilbert, AZ 85296
www.LawleyPublishing.com

LAWLEY
PUBLISHING

Those who knew Harry said he NEVER listened.

His mother called him for
dinner, but he never came.

His teacher called on him to answer a
question, but he never answered.

In PE, the teacher told him to
jump rope, but he never jumped.

His sister would ask him to turn down the
volume of the TV, but he never did.

At the ice cream shop,
they would ask if he
wanted sprinkles, but he
didn't hear them, so his ice
cream was always plain.

"Harry NEVER listens,"
they all said.

One day at school, Harry's teacher announced that they were
all going to the nurse's office to have their hearing checked.

"Everyone will take turns wearing the headphones.
When you hear the beeps raise your hand," the nurse explained.

**When it was Harry's turn, he sat down
and put the headphones over his ears.**

He sat . . .

and sat . . .

and sat.

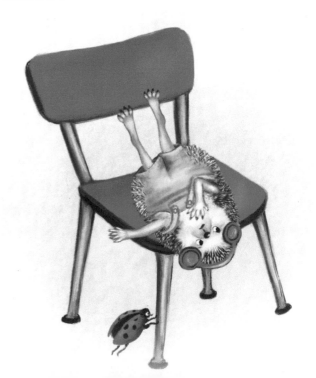

He didn't raise his hand

"Harry NEVER listens," his teacher sighed.

The nurse took off Harry's headphones.
"Remember, Harry, raise your hand when you hear the beeps."

"Okay, but I didn't hear any beeps," Harry said.

"Let's try again,"
said the nurse.

Again Harry sat still, not raising his hand.

The nurse pressed buttons, making the beeps

louder

and

louder.

Finally, when the beeps were loud enough for Harry to hear them, he raised his hand.

When the nurse finished the test, she
had Harry take off the headphones.

"Harry, do you have a hard time hearing
people when they are talking to you?"
asked the nurse.

Harry nodded.

"I think you need hearing aids to help you hear better," she said.

"Really?" Harry asked.

"Really?" asked his teacher.

"Really," said the nurse.

Later that week, Harry's mom
took him to the doctor, where he
was fit with hearing aids.

Harry got to pick his favorite color, bright red.

The doctor whispered,
"Can you hear me?"

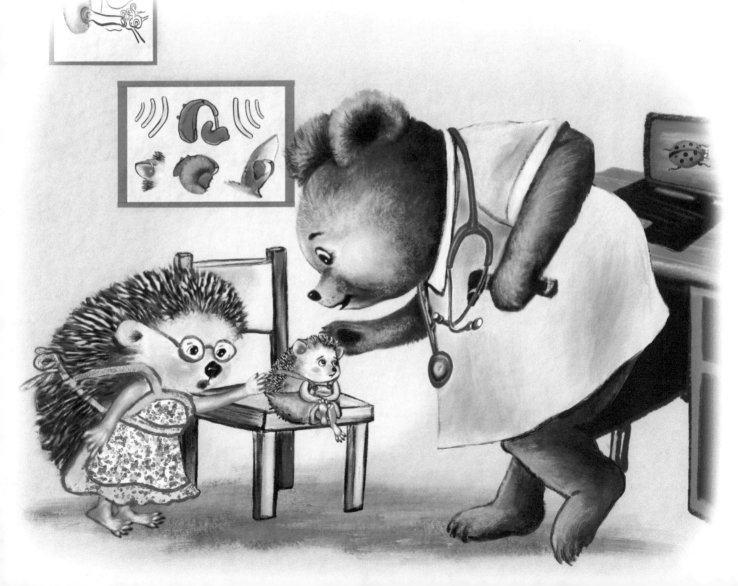

"I can hear you, I can hear you!"
Harry cheered, excited to finally
hear whispers.

When Harry and his mom got home, his sister came running to see his hearing aids.

"Wow, your hearing aids look so cool," his sister said.

Now, when his mother called
him for dinner, he came.

When his teacher called on him to answer a question, he answered.

In PE, when the teacher told him
to jump rope, he jumped.

And he no longer turned the volume up on the TV.

At the ice cream shop,
when they asked if he
wanted sprinkles, he heard
them and chose sprinkles

. . . and whip cream,
chocolate syrup, gummy
bears, chocolate chips,
brownie bites,

and a cherry on top.

Want more insightful, empowering, fun children's books?
Want activities and links to go along with the story?
Visit us at www.lawleypublishing.com

For updates and info on New Releases follow us at

lawleypublishing

@kidsbookswithheart

LAWLEY
PUBLISHING

Printed in the USA
CPSIA information can be obtained
at www.ICGtesting.com
LVHW071948291023
762234LV00023B/76